Unlucky Pony

Do you love ponies? Be a Pony Pal!

PONY PALS

Unlucky Pony

Jeanne Betancourt

illustrated by Susy Boyer Rigby

SCHOLASTIC INC.
New York   Toronto   London   Auckland   Sydney
Mexico City   New Delhi   Hong Kong

ISBN 0-439-06490-2

Text copyright ©1999 by Jeanne Betancourt.
Cover and text illustrations copyright ©1999 by Scholastic Australia. All rights reserved. Published by Scholastic Inc., 555 Broadway, New York, NY 10012, by arrangement with Scholastic Australia Pty Limited.

12 11 10 9 8 7 6 5 4 3 2 1   0 1 2 3 4 5 6/0

Printed in Australia

First Scholastic printing, January 2000
Cover and text illustrations by Susy Boyer Rigby
Typeset in Bookman

Contents

Contents

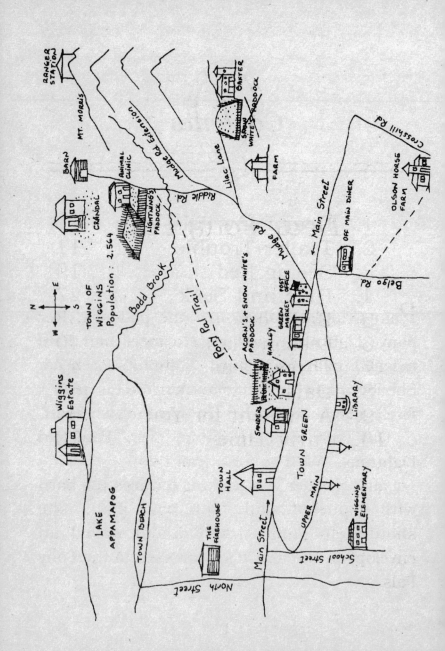

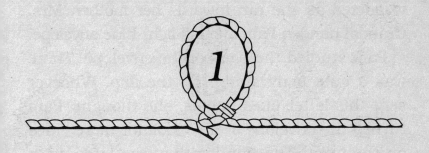

Dear Pony Pals

Pam Crandal walked into the paddock. Her pony, Lightning, ran over to meet her. Pam reached up and scratched Lightning's forehead. She loved how the white marking on her pony's forehead looked just like an upside-down heart.

"Our Pony Pals are coming over," Pam told Lightning. "We'll go for a trail ride."

Pam's mother was walking towards the barn with a pile of mail. "You have mail," she shouted to Pam. Mrs. Crandal waved an envelope in the air. "It's addressed to the Pony Pals."

Who would write a letter to the Pony Pals? Pam wondered as she ran towards her mother. Mrs. Crandal handed Pam a small light-blue envelope.

Pam studied the back of the envelope. There was a cute pony stamp on the flap. Whoever sent this letter likes ponies, she thought. Pam turned the envelope over to look for more clues on the front. The handwriting was large, with big loops. It looked like a grade-school student's writing. There was a return address in the upper left-hand corner.

Eve Greeley
13 Creek Road
Edison, N.Y.

"It's from Eve Greeley," Pam told her mother. "The girl who adopted Lucky. Remember? The baby pony we hand-reared?"

"How could I forget?" her mother said with a laugh. "You girls were busy day and night bottle-feeding that foal. It's a lucky thing you found someone to adopt him."

Pam smiled just thinking about Lucky. "He was so cute," she said.

"And so spoiled," added her mother.

Pam agreed that the orphaned pony *had* been a little spoiled. No matter how much they loved him, they couldn't teach him how to act like a pony. He needed a pony or horse for a mother, not three girls. That was one of the reasons the Pony Pals had searched for a nursing mare to feed him. And they'd found one.

Eve Greeley's father had a horse named Freckles. Freckles had a foal that died when it was born. So Freckles had plenty of milk for nursing the baby pony. The Pony Pals were happy when Freckles accepted the baby pony as her own. But they missed him.

"I can't wait to read Eve's letter," Pam told her mother. "I'm sure it's all about Lucky."

"Well, you won't have to wait for long," Mrs. Crandal said. "Here come Anna and Lulu now."

Pam's Pony Pals galloped off Pony Pal Trail and across the field towards the barn. Pony Pal Trail was a mile-and-a-half-long riding path through the woods. It started at the paddock behind Anna Harley's house and ended at the Crandals'.

Lightning neighed a happy greeting and trotted excitedly along the fence line. Pam ran to meet her friends and their ponies, Snow White and Acorn. She told Pam and Anna about the letter right away.

"Open it," said Lulu as she slid off Snow White.

"And read it to us," added Anna as she jumped off Acorn.

Pam opened the envelope and read the letter out loud.

Dear Pony Pals:
It's me. Eve Greeley. I adopted the baby pony from you. I named him

Lucky. You said that was okay.

Lucky is so cute. He is full of energy. All he wants to do is play and kick and run around. He loves treats.

Do you remember Freckles? She doesn't want to play with Lucky anymore. But Lucky plays with me.

My dad and mom say Lucky is too hard to handle. But I love him. I want to train him, then I can ride him some day.

Can you help me train
Lucky? Please? My
dad says it is okay. Our
telephone number is
354-90000.
Please help Lucky and me.
Your friend,
Eve
PS
Lucky will be one year old
next week.

"It sounds like Lucky is too much for Eve to handle," said Anna.

"It's hard to discipline a pony," said Pam. "Especially if you're just a little kid."

"Maybe we could do it," said Lulu.

"I'd love to see Lucky again," said Anna. "It'd be fun to train him."

"We could try," said Pam. "Let's go and ask my mother if he can come here for training."

Anna and Lulu put their ponies in the paddock and the three girls went to Mrs. Crandal's barn office. They showed her Eve's letter.

When she finished reading it, she sighed. "It sounds like Lucky is too much for Eve to handle," she said.

"They need our help," said Pam. "Can we tell Eve to bring Lucky here?"

"We're on vacation, Mrs. Crandal," Anna pointed out. "So we have time to train him."

Mrs. Crandal looked at her schedule and thought for a minute. "I'll help, too," she told the three girls. "But Lucky and Eve will be your responsibility. Okay?"

"Okay," answered the girls in unison. They were all smiling as they left the office. They couldn't wait to see Lucky again.

Pam pictured the frisky little foal they'd bottle-fed every few hours, night and day.

"He's going to be a lot bigger than he was a year ago," Pam told Lulu and Anna.

"I wonder if he still whinnies when you leave him alone," said Anna.

"And bucks when he's annoyed," said Pam.

"And nips to get attention," added Lulu.

"I bet he's doing all of those things," said Pam. "It's going to be hard work to train him."

"I wonder if he'll remember us," said Anna.

"Let's call Eve right now," suggested Lulu. "Maybe she and Lucky can come tomorrow."

The girls went into the tack room to use the barn phone. Pam dialed the Greeleys' phone number. First she talked to Eve. Eve was excited that the Pony Pals were inviting her and Lucky for a visit.

Next, Pam talked to Mr. Greeley. "My mother said Lucky can stay for three days and two nights," Pam explained. "Eve, too. Eve can have sleepovers with us in the barn. And we'll work with Lucky a lot. Is that okay?"

"It sounds like a good plan," Mr. Greeley answered. "Eve is on vacation, too. Let's see, I can leave here with them around one o'clock tomorrow. So we'll be at your place by two o'clock. Okay?"

"We'll be waiting for you," said Pam.

"Thank your mother for me," concluded Mr. Greeley. "Lucky's so big, I'm afraid Eve could get hurt. This will be his last chance with us."

As Pam hung up the phone, questions popped into her head. Would they be able to train Lucky in two days? Would Eve learn how to handle him? Would she have to give him up? But right now, the biggest question was: How do you train a spoiled one-year-old colt?

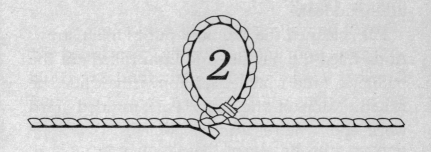

Trailer Trouble

"Lucky and Eve are coming tomorrow," Pam reported to Lulu and Anna.

"Eve can sleep in the barn with us. I told her to bring her sleeping bag."

"Can Lucky stay in the paddock with our ponies?" asked Anna.

"Not at first," answered Pam. "They might not remember him."

"And it sounds like he's misbehaving," added Lulu.

"Let's put him back in his old stall,"

suggested Pam. "It's empty and has its own little paddock."

Pam cleaned the stall and put in fresh straw. Anna filled the hay net and Lulu raked out the paddock. Lulu whistled a happy tune while she raked. None of the Pony Pals minded hard work—not when it was for ponies.

Pam remembered how hard it had been to take care of Lucky when he was a baby. At first the Pony Pals didn't know if they could keep the motherless foal alive. They were all worried about him, especially Lulu. Pam thought that was because Lulu's mother had died when she was little.

Lulu's father traveled all over the world studying wild animals. After her mother died, he took Lulu with him on the trips. But when Lulu turned ten he said she should live in one place. That's when Lulu moved to her grandmother's house in Wiggins. At first Lulu thought the small town would be boring after all her exciting trips. Then she met Anna and Pam and their ponies. Lulu had found Snow White in a field, caught in barbed wire. She'd helped her and now Snow White was her very own pony. Living in Wiggins had turned out to be the greatest adventure of all.

Anna and Pam had lived in Wiggins all their lives. They'd been best friends since meeting in kindergarten. Pam had her own pony for as long as she could remember. But Anna didn't have her own pony until she was ten years old. Before that she rode ponies at the Crandals'. Pam's mother was a riding teacher, so Anna took lessons with her.

The one thing Pam and Anna disagreed about was reading and writing. Pam loved to read big books and write compositions. But Anna was dyslexic, so reading and writing were difficult for her. She preferred to draw and paint pictures. Pam thought Anna was a great artist.

Lulu came back into the stall. "The yard's cleaned up," she announced.

Anna fluffed up the hay net. "And here's a nice big snack for Lucky," she said.

"And his stall is all clean and cosy," added Pam.

Lulu looked at her watch. "It's two o'clock

13

now," she said. "Lucky will be here in twenty-four hours. What do we have to do next?"

"Figure out how to train him," said Pam. "Let's talk to my mom and look at her books on training yearlings."

The three girls ran back to the barn office to prepare for their student.

The next morning the Pony Pals went for a trail ride and picnic. It was their last chance to relax alone with their ponies. Soon they'd be responsible for Lucky and Eve.

They were back at the Crandals' before two o'clock.

"Let's practice jumping cross rails until they come," suggested Pam. "They're already set up in the ring."

The three girls rode into the riding ring and took turns jumping a small course of eighteen-inch-high cross rails.

At two-thirty the Greeleys still hadn't arrived.

"How long does it take to drive from Edison to Wiggins?" Lulu asked Pam.

"About a half hour," Pam answered. "Or maybe a little longer with a horse trailer."

"Here comes your father, Pam," Anna called from the other end of the course.

Dr. Crandal was talking on his cell phone as he hurried towards them. Pam rode Lightning out of the riding ring to meet him. Lulu and Anna followed on their ponies.

"What's wrong?" Pam asked her father when she reached him.

Dr. Crandal couldn't answer because he was still talking on the phone. "I understand," he said into the phone. "Someone will be there soon. We'll find him."

"What's happened?" asked Pam.

"That was the state trooper," Dr. Crandal answered. "The Greeleys were in an accident. A truck passed too close and hit the side of their car. On Riddle Road, where it meets Lilac Lane. No one was seriously hurt."

"Is Lucky okay?" asked Pam.

"The trooper said Lucky had a cut on his front left leg."

"Who do you have to find?" Pam asked. "You said you had to find someone."

"Lucky," her father answered. "In the excitement after the accident, Lucky ran away."

"What about Eve and her father?" asked Lulu. "Are they okay?"

"The ambulance took them to the hospital," Dr. Crandal said. "To be checked for injuries."

Pam turned to Lulu and Anna. "We have to find Lucky," she said.

"I think you girls are the best ones to do it," said Dr. Crandal. "I'd go with you, but I'm in surgery. I was on my way into the operating room when the trooper phoned."

Dr. Crandal handed Pam his cell phone. "Take this. Call the clinic with any news or if you need help. I should be out of surgery in an hour. If we haven't heard from you by then, I'll call you." He turned and rushed back to the clinic.

"Do you still have the first aid kit in your saddle bag?" Lulu asked Pam.

Pam nodded.

"I have the binoculars," added Anna.

"And I have wire clippers," Lulu told them. "In case Lucky gets caught in a barbed wire fence."

"And we all have our whistles," said Pam. She gave Lightning a tap with her heel. "Let's go."

Pam and Lightning led the way out of the driveway onto Riddle Road. Poor Lucky, thought Pam. He's frightened, injured and running wild.

How bad was his wound? she wondered. Was it still bleeding? Would they find him before he hurt himself even more? And what about Eve and her father? Were they going to be okay?

Pam moved Lightning into a gallop. The sooner they reached the accident site, the sooner they could start looking for Lucky.

Seeing Red

Pam and Lightning reached the Greeleys' car first. Lulu and Anna were right behind her on their ponies.

The Greeleys' station wagon was badly scraped and dented. The horse trailer doors were open.

A big white truck was parked on the other side of the road. A state trooper was talking to the truck driver and writing notes. Another trooper was walking towards the Pony Pals. Pam recognized her. It was Officer Hunter.

The three girls dismounted. Lulu handed

Snow White's reins to Pam. "I'll go and look for clues," Lulu said.

"We'll wait here," said Pam. "Too many footprints could destroy evidence."

Officer Hunter said hello to Pam and Anna. She knew them, too.

"Dr. Crandal sent us to find the runaway pony," said Anna.

"I called the local animal rescue agency," Officer Hunter told them. "But they can't get here for at least an hour."

"I hope we find Lucky before that," said Pam. "He must be so confused and frightened."

Lulu was running to her friends and Officer Hunter.

"I found hoof prints," she said breathlessly. "They lead to Lilac Lane. He went that way."

"Let's ride," said Pam. "It'll be faster. Lulu, you lead."

Lulu was already back in the saddle.

Pam and Anna followed Lulu onto Lilac Lane. Lulu stopped suddenly. Pam and Anna halted their ponies behind her.

"Look," said Lulu as she pointed to the ground in front of her.

Pam saw the imprint of a small pony hoof track in the dirt road.

"It's wet," Lulu said.

"It's probably blood," said Pam. "From the cut."

"That's a lot of blood!" gasped Anna.

"We have to hurry," said Lulu as she moved Snow White back into motion.

Soon the dirt road ended. So did Lucky's hoof prints.

"I forgot that Lilac Lane is a dead end," said Anna.

"Which way did he go?" asked Pam.

"He could have gone to the left," answered Lulu. "Into the woods. Or to the right, through farm fields."

"Let's look for clues," suggested Anna. "But hurry. Before he gets too far ahead of us."

Or bleeds to death, thought Pam.

The three girls dismounted. Lulu and Anna looked for clues along the edge of the woods that went to Mount Morris. Pam led Lightning over to the farmland side of the road. She looked all along the side of the road for tracks. She didn't find any.

Suddenly, Lightning stopped to sniff a clump of grass.

"We don't have time for snacking," Pam told her.

Lightning nickered and pulled on the reins. She wasn't trying to eat grass. Pam went over to see what Lightning was sniffing.

Something dark red stuck to the grass. Pam rubbed it off with her fingers. It was blood.

"Lightning's found something," Pam shouted to Anna and Lulu. She patted Lightning's neck. "Good work, Lightning," she said.

Lulu found more blood-stained grass. "Lucky went this way," she said.

The three girls rode across the field. They came to a barn and a farm house at the other end.

"Maybe someone at this farm saw him," Pam called to Lulu and Anna. "Let's ask."

As the three girls were dismounting, a tall,

thin man rushed out of the barn. He was carrying a big coil of thick rope.

"Who are you?" he shouted. "What do you want?"

Pam put an arm around Lightning's shoulder. "I'm Pam Crandal," she said.

Anna and Lulu quickly introduced themselves, too.

"Did you see a runaway pony?" Pam asked the man.

"He's brown and injured," added Lulu.

The man pointed towards a field of tall corn behind the barn. "He ran into the cornfield," he said.

"We've been looking for him," said Pam.

"Just what I need," the farmer hissed. "A bunch of kids getting in the way. I'll take care of it." He turned to go into the cornfield.

Pam imagined how the thick, rough rope would feel on the little pony's neck. The man didn't care if Lucky was injured and bleeding.

Pam looked the farmer right in the eye. "We know a lot about ponies," Pam told him. "We'll help."

A crashing noise came from the cornfield. Pam saw a flash of brown. Lucky was still there. A frightened pony could trip on that bumpy ground, thought Pam. Or catch a hoof on a corn stalk. He could break a leg.

"I'm going to catch him before he ruins my corn!" said the angry man. "I'll teach him."

"Stop!" shouted Pam. "Let me try to catch him."

"Is he yours?" the man asked.

Pam remembered how she'd saved the pony's life by bottle-feeding him. The Pony Pals had been his mother for the first few weeks of his life.

"Yes," she said. "His name is Lucky."

"And if you hurt him there'll be big trouble," said Lulu.

"I'll give you five minutes," the man said. The corners of his mouth turned up in an evil grin. "And since it's your pony, you're responsible for the damage to my corn crop."

Pam handed Lightning's reins to Lulu. "I'll get him," said Pam.

"I'll help," said Anna.

"I'll take care of the ponies," said Lulu.

Pam took a lead rope from her saddle bag and tied it around her waist. She'd need it for Lucky. She pointed to her right. "I'll go this way," she told Anna. "You go around the other side. Don't charge at him. Be gentle and quiet."

"I will," said Anna as she handed Acorn's reins to Lulu.

As Pam headed into the tall corn she wondered if they really could catch Lucky.

Hide and Seek

Pam walked slowly and quietly between the rows of tall corn. There was a thrashing sound to her right. She knew it was Lucky, but she still couldn't see him.

Pam remembered singing lullabies to the baby pony when she first fed him his bottle. I'll do that now, she thought. By the time she finished the first verse of "All the Pretty Horses," the thrashing noise stopped. Pam kept singing.

Finally she spotted the pony through the stalks of corn. His ears were tilted towards her. He's listening, she thought. Pam continued singing as she moved towards the pony. As she came closer she saw patches of dried blood on the pony's leg. She realized that Lucky might be wounded very badly.

At that instant Lucky saw Pam. He turned and ran away from her again. He's afraid of everyone now, thought Pam. But I bet he's not afraid of other ponies. Ponies are always curious about other ponies. Maybe Lucky will come close to Lightning.

Pam ran back out of the field.

"I knew you couldn't do it," the farmer said. "Singing lullabies! Are you playing dolls or catching a dumb animal?"

"Lucky's not dumb," Lulu mumbled under her breath. "And the five minutes aren't up."

"If that were my pony I'd sing him a lullaby he wouldn't forget," said the farmer. "Then he'd behave and wouldn't be running off." He sneered at Pam. "You'll learn."

Pam didn't waste time answering the farmer. She'd met people like him before—people who didn't respect or understand animals.

"I'm going to take Lightning in there," Pam

told Lulu. "Lucky might stop running away when he sees another pony."

"Good idea," agreed Lulu.

As Pam was leading Lightning into the cornfield she had another idea. If she was riding Lightning she'd be higher and she'd have a better view. Pam swung up onto Lightning's back.

To her left she saw Anna walking quietly through the cornfield, looking for Lucky. To her right she saw Lucky. He'd stopped running. His head was lifted and he was sniffing the air. He can smell Lightning, thought Pam.

Lucky made a little nickering sound.

Lightning whinnied.

Lucky took a few steps in Lightning's direction.

Pam gave Lightning a loose rein and quietly slid off her. Lightning moved towards Lucky. Anna was coming towards Lucky from the other direction. The two ponies sniffed curiously at one another.

Pam ran up to Lucky and clipped the lead rope on his halter. Lucky quickly turned his head and nipped Pam's hand.

Pam looked down at Lucky's front left leg. There was dried blood down one side, but the cut wasn't bleeding anymore. She still couldn't tell how badly he was injured.

"You lead Lightning out first," Pam told Anna. "I think Lucky will follow her."

Anna and Lightning led the way through the field. Pam and Lucky followed. Pam watched how Lucky walked. He wasn't limping.

Lulu and the farmer were waiting for them near the barn. Pam stopped and held the pony tight. She wasn't going to let him run away again.

"I'll send you a bill for the corn," the farmer said. "Now get off my land."

"I have to call my father first," Pam told the man. "And tell him that Lucky is safe."

Lulu held Lucky's lead rope while Pam used the cell phone. Lucky tried to escape from her by pushing into her and pulling away, but Lulu held on.

Pam's father answered the phone. Pam told him that they had found Lucky and that the cut was on his lower leg. "It's not bleeding anymore," she reported. "And he's not limping."

"Head on home with him," instructed Dr. Crandal. "But if he starts to limp, stop and call me."

Next, Pam asked her father if Eve and Mr. Greeley were okay. He said he didn't know. "Your mother is at the hospital now," he said.

After Pam hung up, she told Anna and Lulu everything her father had said. "It would be too scary for Lucky to be in a trailer now," she concluded. "So we'll walk him back."

The farmer shook his head. "You're spoiling that pony rotten," he grumbled. He turned and headed into his cornfield.

"Why don't you take Lucky," Lulu told Pam. "And I can lead Lightning with Snow White."

"Good plan," said Pam. "Anna, you and Acorn take up the rear."

Lucky calmed down as soon as they started moving. He wanted to keep up with the other ponies.

As they headed across the open field, Pam kept an eye on Lucky. He'd grown a lot in one year. And already she could tell he was very spoiled. She wondered how the Pony Pals could turn him into a well-behaved pony. What would happen to Lucky if they failed?

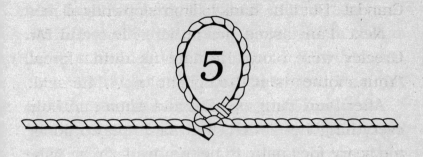

Bad Pony

Half an hour later the parade of girls and ponies reached the Crandals'.

Eve ran out to meet them. Dr. Crandal, Mrs. Crandal and Mr. Greeley were right behind her.

"Lucky! Lucky!" Eve cried as she ran towards them.

Mr. Greeley had a bruise on his left cheek and an ace bandage on his wrist.

"Are you okay, Mr. Greeley?" Anna asked.

"It looks worse than it is," said Mr. Greeley. "And Eve isn't hurt at all."

"I'm so glad," said Lulu.

Eve threw her arms around Lucky's neck and kissed him. Lucky lowered his head and pulled at her jeans' jacket with his teeth. Eve reached in her pocket and pulled out a small apple. "Here's your treat," she told him.

Anna and Pam exchanged a glance. Always expecting treats was a sign of a spoiled pony.

Mr. Greeley patted Lucky's head. "Now, what about this little fellow?"

Dr. Crandal was already inspecting Lucky's injured leg. "It's not a deep cut," he said. "He'll be fine. Pam, you and Eve bring him to the barn and we'll clean it up."

"Lulu and I can take care of Lightning," Anna told Pam.

"Thanks," said Pam.

As Pam and Eve walked Lucky towards the barn, Pam noticed that Eve was still crying.

"Lucky's going to be all right," Pam told her. "He's safe now."

"It's my fault he ran away," Eve sobbed. "I didn't take care of him."

"It was the middle of an accident," Pam told her. "Everything was all confused."

Eve looked up at Pam. There were still tears in her eyes.

"Lucky is a handful," Pam told her. "I had trouble with him, too."

Eve nodded.

"That's why you're here," Pam continued, "so we can all train him."

They led Lucky into the new barn. Dr. Crandal was waiting for them. Eve and Pam watched while he cleaned the cut and smeared medicine on it.

"After some food and a little rest he'll be good as new," Dr. Crandal said.

"Come on, Eve," Pam told the little girl. "We'll put him in his stall and feed him."

Lulu and Anna met them at Lucky's stall.

When Lucky was settled down, the four girls went back to the house. Mr. and Mrs. Greeley were sitting at the kitchen table with Pam's mother.

Mrs. Greeley got up and ran over to hug Eve. "My poor baby," she cried. "Are you really okay?"

"Lucky got hurt," answered Eve. "And he ran away!"

"That pony should have been named *Trouble* instead of *Lucky*," complained Mrs. Greeley.

"Training a yearling isn't easy," Mrs. Crandal told the Greeleys. "You have your hands full with Lucky."

"He's been a lot more work than we expected," said Mrs. Greeley. "Especially since he's stopped nursing."

"Before that Freckles was taking care of him," explained Mr. Greeley. "She was teaching him how to behave while she was giving him milk. But when the nursing stopped, they had to be separated for a while. Now Freckles doesn't want to be bothered with a frisky pony. And I don't have time."

"He's been very busy at work," Mrs. Greeley explained.

"And you have a new job," Mr. Greeley said.

"But even if I had time," Mrs. Greeley added, "I'm not that interested in ponies." She smiled at Eve. "I prefer little girls. And cats. I like cats."

I'm so lucky that both my parents love ponies and horses as much as I do, thought Pam.

"We'll train him, Mrs. Greeley," said Anna. "It'll be fun."

"And we'll teach Eve how to work with him," added Pam. She turned to her mother. "Mom said she'd help."

"And I will," said Mrs. Crandal. "I just hope you all realize that training a yearling can be difficult."

"We know," the Pony Pals answered in unison.

"But if Eve can't learn to control him, she won't be able to keep him," said Mr Greeley.

"I *will*," said Eve. "The Pony Pals are going to teach me."

"We're going to *try*," Pam reminded her.

After Eve's parents left, Eve and the Pony Pals had a snack of cookies and juice. Then they went back to the barn to check on Lucky.

When Eve opened the stall door, Lucky ran over to her. He poked her pocket with his nose so hard that she almost fell over.

"Don't worry," Eve told Lucky. "I have a treat for you." Eve took a piece of carrot from her pocket and gave it to the pony.

He gobbled it down, turned, and ran out the back door to his little paddock.

"Eve," said Pam, "do you always give Lucky a treat when you see him?"

Eve nodded.

"You're going to have to stop doing that if you want to train him to be good," said Lulu.

"No more treats," said Anna.

"But then he'll bite me," protested Eve.

"We'll have to teach him to stop biting you, too," said Lulu.

"And not to push you around," said Pam.

"How?" asked Eve.

"Let's have a Pony Pal Meeting to plan lessons for Lucky," suggested Lulu.

"Can I come to the meeting?" asked Eve. "Am I a Pony Pal?"

"You're a junior Pony Pal," said Pam. "And it's very important that you come to the meeting. We're all going to have to work together to train Lucky."

"Or else my mom and dad won't let me keep him," said Eve sadly.

Lulu and Pam exchanged a worried glance. Could they turn Lucky into a well-behaved pony?

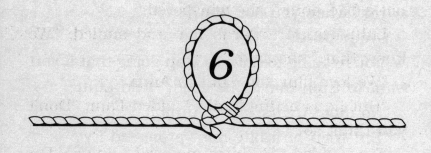

Lesson Plan

The Pony Pals and Eve climbed the ladder to the hayloft. The four girls sat around the haybale table.

"Pam, you start the meeting," suggested Anna.

"Okay," agreed Pam. "This is a Pony Pal Meeting to talk about training Lucky."

Lulu took out her notebook. "I'll write down what we decide at this meeting."

"Eve, you tell us a problem you have with Lucky," suggested Anna. "Then we can all talk about how to fix it."

Eve nervously picked at the hay table. "He's not a bad pony," she whispered.

Lulu leaned towards her and smiled. "We know that," she said.

"We love him, too," put in Anna.

"But he is acting badly," added Pam. "Don't you think so?"

Eve nodded. "He bites me a lot," she said.

"That's because he's always expecting a treat," said Pam. "You should stop giving him treats."

"Only give him food at meal times," added Lulu. "And never feed him from your hands."

"What else does he do that he shouldn't?" asked Anna.

"He pushes me," answered Eve. "Once he stepped on my foot. It hurt."

"If he pushes you, Eve, elbow him," suggested Anna. "You have to be firm with him."

"My mother said she'd work with him on leading and halting," Pam told Eve. "When he learns those two things he'll be better behaved."

"What else does he do that you don't like?" asked Lulu.

"Sometimes he scares me," said Eve in a soft

voice. "I think he's going to kick me." She looked up at Pam. "I'm even afraid to brush him."

"We'll work on grooming him," said Pam. "If we do a little at a time, he'll get used to it."

They talked about the problems with Lucky some more. Lulu made a list of what they decided. Pam read the list out loud.

TRAINING LUCKY
Many short grooming sessions
No treats
No feeding from hands
Don't let him push you
Be firm
A lesson on handling and leading with Mrs. Crandal

"Let's tack this list outside his stall," suggested Anna. "To remind us what we have to do."

"And let's have a short grooming session now," said Lulu.

"Good idea," agreed Pam. "But remember, just brush him a little." She stood up. "I'm going to tell my mother what we discussed. I'll meet you at Lucky's stall."

Pam found her mother in the barn office. She reported what Eve had said about Lucky.

"He's been getting away with some very bad pony behavior," her mother said. "But we should wait until tomorrow to work with him. He's had enough excitement for one day."

"Okay," agreed Pam.

Pam went back to Lucky's stall. Lulu was holding Lucky's lead rope. Eve was brushing his coat. The little pony suddenly tried to pull away from Lulu. He nickered as if to say, "Leave me alone."

"Ouch!" shouted Eve. She jumped back. "He stepped on my foot."

Lulu pulled on Lucky's lead rope and said, "Whoa."

"He doesn't like to stay still," said Anna.

"It's my fault," said Eve. "I spoiled him."

"It's nobody's fault," said Pam. "I think we should leave Lucky alone for now."

Lulu let the pony free. He turned and ran out to his paddock.

Pam looked at her watch. "It's almost time for dinner," she said. "We're having spaghetti."

Anna put an arm around Eve. "Wait until you taste Dr. Crandal's spaghetti sauce," she said.

"He makes amazing meatballs," added Pam.

"Eve, do you like spaghetti and meatballs?" asked Lulu.

"It's my favorite," said Eve. But she didn't sound very happy.

On the way to the house, Lulu told Eve that she'd be meeting Pam's brother and sister.

"They're twins," explained Pam. "A girl and a boy. They're five years old."

"Their names are Jack and Jill," added Anna.

Eve finally smiled when she heard the twins' names.

After dinner and dishes, Eve, the Pony Pals and the twins watched a video of "Black Beauty." Pam noticed that Eve cried the most during the movie. She really loves horses, thought Pam.

When the movie was over, Lulu yawned and stretched her arms. "I'm tired," she said.

"And we have to get up early," added Anna. "We only have two days to train Lucky."

By nine o'clock the four girls were in sleeping bags in the hayloft. Before long Pam heard Anna's slow, even breathing. She was asleep. Next, Pam heard Lulu's little snores.

Pam heard another sound in the dark. Someone was crying. And it was coming from Eve's sleeping bag.

Pam slipped out of her sleeping bag and crawled over to Eve. In the moonlight, she could see that Eve's eyes were closed. She wasn't crying anymore and her breath was slow and even.

She's cried herself to sleep, thought Pam sadly. She pulled the top of the sleeping bag up around Eve's shoulders.

Pam went back to her own sleeping bag. She stared at the starry sky through the hayloft window. Is it our fault that Eve is upset? she wondered. Is she too young to train a pony? Training Lucky and helping Eve was turning into a bigger problem than she thought.

It was time for three ideas.

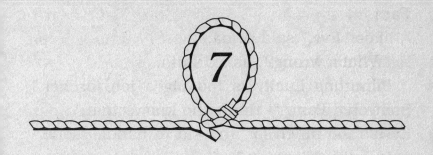

Three Ideas

Pam woke up early the next morning. She sat up and looked around the hayloft. Anna was waking up, too. Pam went over to her. "I want to have an emergency Pony Pal Meeting," she whispered. "Without Eve."

Next, Pam woke up Lulu and told her about the meeting.

The three friends quietly left the hayloft. At the bottom of the ladder, Pam signaled them to follow her into the barn office. She closed the door and faced them.

"What's up?" asked Lulu.

"Eve cried herself to sleep last night," said Pam.

"Poor Eve," said Anna.

"What's wrong?" asked Lulu.

"Training Lucky is too big a job for her," answered Pam. "I think she knows that."

"It's too much for any kid to handle alone," said Lulu. "Even us."

"Eve's parents don't have time to help her," said Anna. "And her mother doesn't even like ponies."

"But Eve loves him," said Lulu. "He's her pony."

"It's a big problem," concluded Pam. "Let's all think of a solution. After Lucky's lesson with my mom this morning, we'll have another secret meeting about Eve and Lucky."

The Pony Pals climbed back up the ladder to the hayloft. It was time to get dressed and wake up Eve.

The four girls fed their ponies. Then they went to the house for breakfast.

After breakfast they walked back to the barn. It was time for Lucky's first lesson of the day.

Pam saw Acorn and Snow White resting under the big maple tree. She looked around for her own pony. Lightning was on the other side of the paddock. Her head hung over the fence separating the big paddock and Lucky's little paddock. Lucky was sniffing Lightning's face.

Eve noticed them, too. "Look at Lightning and Lucky!" she exclaimed.

"They're making friends," said Lulu.

Seeing the two ponies together gave Pam an idea. She quickly took out her notebook and wrote it down.

The four girls went over to the fence to watch Mrs. Crandal work with Lucky. "Do you want me to help?" Pam called to her mother.

"Not yet," her mother answered.

The first thing Mrs. Crandal did was put a halter on Lucky. The pony nipped at the halter.

"He doesn't like halters," Eve told Pam.

Mrs. Crandal spoke firmly to Lucky and didn't let him take over. When he pushed into her, she pushed him away. When he reared, she disciplined him. Next, she taught him to walk and halt.

Pam noticed that during the lesson, Anna took out her pocket sketch pad and did a little drawing.

"That's enough for now, girls," Mrs. Crandal said. "We'll work with him again this afternoon, after my last class. Meet me here at five."

"Thanks, Mom," Pam called.

Pam saw Lulu quickly write down something in her notebook. Pam wondered what Lulu's idea was. It was time to distract Eve so the Pony Pals could have a meeting to share their ideas.

"I'm thirsty," Pam announced. "Eve, can you go to the house and get us some juice? There's a big jug in the refrigerator."

"Okay," agreed Eve.

As soon as Eve was gone, the Pony Pals stood in a little circle outside the paddock.

"I didn't know training a yearling was so hard!" exclaimed Anna.

"It's even hard for your mom," added Lulu.

"Lucky's going to have to learn how to behave really fast," said Pam. "Otherwise Eve won't be able to keep him."

"Let's share our ideas about what to do," said Anna, "before Eve gets back."

Lulu showed her idea to Pam and Anna.

DAISY

"Daisy?" asked Anna. "Mrs. Crandal's school pony?"

"I think that Eve should have a lesson on Daisy," said Lulu. "Half the fun of having a pony is riding. Eve needs to have some fun with ponies."

"Daisy would be perfect for Eve to ride," said Anna. "Daisy's very well trained and calm."

"Riding Daisy will give Eve confidence," suggested Pam. "And show her that she can control a pony."

"Exactly," said Lulu. "What's your idea, Pam?"

Pam reached into her jeans' pocket and pulled out her Pony Pal notebook and read:

Lucky should be with the other ponies.

"A yearling needs to be around other ponies,"

explained Pam. "That's how they learn pony behavior."

"Lightning likes Lucky," said Pam. "Let's put them together in the small paddock."

"Lightning has a lot to teach him about how to behave," said Anna.

"Good idea, Pam," said Lulu. "What's your idea, Anna?" asked Lulu.

Anna opened a folded piece of paper and showed it to Pam and Lulu.

"A birthday party for Lucky!" exclaimed Lulu. "That's such a good idea."

"We can invite Rosalie and Mimi," said Anna. "They love ponies."

"Let's have the party tomorrow afternoon," suggested Pam. "Eve's parents can come, too."

"Eve hasn't been having much fun with ponies lately," said Pam. "But having a lesson on Daisy and planning a party will be great fun."

Eve was coming towards them with a big jar of juice and paper cups. Anna ran to help her.

All of our ideas were good, thought Pam. But they didn't solve the biggest problem of all. Would Eve be able to keep Lucky?

Daisy

Pam took the jug of juice from Eve. Anna held out the paper cups for Pam to pour.

"Eve, do you still take riding lessons?" asked Pam.

"Not anymore," answered Eve.

"How come?" asked Lulu.

"Lucky's my pony," answered Eve. "But he's not ready for me to ride. I have to wait until he grows up."

"You won't be able to ride Lucky for years," said Pam.

Anna handed Eve a juice. "Do you miss riding?" she asked.

Eve nodded.

"It's important for you to keep up your riding skills," Pam told Eve. "It will make you a better trainer for Lucky."

"You could ride today," suggested Lulu. "On Daisy. She's a great little school pony."

"I have to train Lucky today," said Eve. "To make him behave better. Remember?"

"We're going to let Lightning take care of Lucky for a while," said Pam. "She'll show him how a pony is supposed to act."

Lulu turned to Eve. "Let's go to the barn and talk to Mrs. Crandal about letting you ride Daisy," she said. "Then I'll help you saddle up."

"And I'll put Lightning and Lucky together in the small paddock," said Pam.

Eve turned to Anna. "What are you going to do?" she asked.

Anna smiled at Eve. "I have phone calls to make," she said. "I'm inviting some friends to a birthday party tomorrow afternoon."

"A birthday party!" exclaimed Eve. "Am I invited?"

"Oh, yes," said Pam. "It's very important for you to be there."

Lulu and Pam smiled at one another. So far their ideas were working.

"Whose birthday party is it?" Eve asked excitedly. "Is it yours, Anna?"

Anna shook her head.

"Whose?" asked Eve.

"Lucky's!" exclaimed Anna. "We're going to have a birthday party for Lucky because he's one year old."

Eve jumped up and down excitedly. "Yeah!" she shouted.

Lucky nickered as if to say, "Hey, what's going on?"

"You're going to have a birthday party," Eve shouted to him.

Eve ran over to Lucky and gave him a big hug. Lucky lowered his head and let Eve pat him on the nose.

"Come on, Eve," said Lulu. "Let's go and ask Mrs. Crandal about Daisy."

"Tell her about the party," said Pam. "My brother and sister should come, too."

"I'll go call Mimi and Rosalie and invite them to the party," Anna said.

"Who are they?" asked Eve.

"They're a little younger than you, but lots of fun," answered Lulu.

"And they're both pony-crazy," added Pam.

Lulu, Anna and Eve went into the barn.

Pam went into the big paddock to get Lightning. Lightning came over when Pam called her.

"I have a pony-sitting job for you," she told Lightning.

Lightning nuzzled Pam's shoulder. Pam patted her pony's cheek. "It's a tough job, but I know you can do it," she said.

Pam led Lightning into a paddock on the other side of Lucky's little yard. Lucky watched curiously.

"Okay, Lightning," Pam told her pony. "I'm bringing him in."

Pam opened the gate between the two paddocks. Lucky ran through the opening and stopped a few feet from Lightning. Lightning ignored the yearling.

Lucky walked a little closer.

Lightning nickered a friendly greeting.

Lucky ran right up to Lightning and nipped Lightning on the side.

Lightning turned and made a squeal that said, "Watch yourself." Then she nipped Lucky on the rump.

Pam hoped that Lucky was learning his lesson.

Lightning squealed at the little pony one more time. Then she turned her back on him and walked over to the other side of the paddock.

Lucky looked around. He was deciding what to do next. He took a few steps forward and pawed the ground. Lightning ignored him. He took another few steps towards Lightning.

Lightning looked up and nodded. Lucky ran all the way over to Lightning, but this time he didn't nip or kick. Soon the two ponies were grazing peacefully side by side.

Pam left them and went over to the riding

ring. Anna was leaning on the fence watching Eve ride Daisy. Lulu and Mrs. Crandal were in the center of the ring.

"Mimi and Rosalie can come," Anna told Pam. "Mrs. Bell said she'd bring them. Tongo, too. They're going to come over on Pony Pal Trail."

Mrs. Bell was Mimi Kline's babysitter and Tongo was Mimi's pony.

"A pony coming to a pony's party," said Pam. "That's great."

Pam watched Eve and Daisy circle the ring twice. Eve followed all of Mrs. Crandal's directions perfectly. She halted Daisy, moved her from a walk to a trot. She even cantered.

Pam smiled to herself. Eve was a good rider.

When Eve's lesson was over, Eve and Lulu went back into the barn with Daisy.

Mrs. Crandal came over to Pam and Anna at the fence.

"Eve looked good riding," Pam said.

"She's a terrific little rider," agreed Mrs.

Crandal. "But she can't train that frisky yearling all on her own."

"I know," said Pam.

"Her parents are going to ask us what we think," Mrs. Crandal added sadly. "We'll have to tell them the truth."

"They won't let her keep Lucky," said Anna. "They'll sell him or give him away and she'll never see him again. That's so sad."

It is sad, thought Pam.

That evening the Pony Pals and Eve ate dinner on the picnic rock and planned Lucky's party.

"Let's have a chocolate horseshoe cake," suggested Anna. "I'll make it."

"How do you make a horseshoe cake?" asked Eve.

"In a circle pan," explained Anna. "You just cut off part of the bottom and you have a horseshoe."

"It will be a Lucky horseshoe cake," said Eve with a giggle. "Can I help decorate it?"

"You can help me make the party hats, too," said Anna.

"Goodie!" exclaimed Eve.

Pam was glad to see Eve happy. She wished the happiness could last. But she knew it couldn't. Tomorrow Eve would learn that she couldn't keep Lucky.

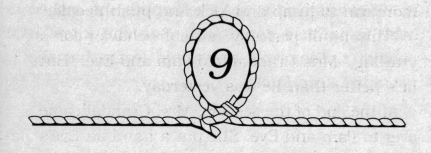

9

A Present for You

The next morning Anna and Lulu prepared for the party, while Pam and Eve watched Mrs. Crandal train Lucky.

The training session was in the riding ring. Lucky shook his head when Mrs. Crandal was putting on the halter. But after pushing Mrs. Crandal, trying to nip her and pawing the ground, he calmed down. She clipped on the lead line and worked on leading and halting.

Pam saw that Lucky was making progress. But he still didn't want to pay attention and do what he was told. He thought it was much more fun to jump and kick and push people.

"This is all perfectly normal behavior for a yearling," Mrs. Crandal told Pam and Eve. "But he's better than he was yesterday."

At the end of the session, Mrs. Crandal came over to Pam and Eve. She put a hand on Eve's shoulders. "Your mother and father will be here around two," she said. "Then we'll have to talk about what to do with Lucky."

Eve nodded. Pam noticed that she looked sad and worried.

"Let's put Lucky back with Lightning now," Pam suggested. "It's Lightning's turn to be his teacher."

Pam and Eve opened the gate between the two paddocks. Lucky went over to Eve and she patted his head. "Go play with your friend," she told him.

The colt nickered happily and ran over to the bigger pony.

Lightning squealed as if to say, "There you are."

"Let's go and help decorate the cake," Pam told Eve. "I bet it's ready."

"Okay," agreed Eve.

A few minutes later Pam and Eve walked into the kitchen. A circle cake was cooling on the counter.

The kitchen table was covered with art supplies. Anna was gluing silver sparkles onto a blue paper hat. Lulu was folding pink paper to make another hat.

"The cake smells great!" exclaimed Pam.

"It has to cool before we decorate it," announced Lulu.

"Come and help us make hats," Anna told Eve and Pam.

"You know that *special thing* we were waiting for, Pam," said Lulu mysteriously. "It's here."

"What special thing?" asked Eve.

"We have a present for you," said Anna. "Mrs. Crandal picked it up for us in town."

Pam grinned. "We can't tell you what it is," she told Eve. "It's a surprise."

Pam noticed that Eve didn't smile or act excited about the present. Instead she picked up a piece of yellow construction paper, a black magic marker and some ribbon. "I have a present for you, too," she explained. "I'm going to go make it now."

Eve turned and left the room. The Pony Pals looked at one another.

"She knows her parents won't let her keep Lucky," said Pam.

"She's trying to be brave," said Anna. "She's even making us a present."

"I feel so sorry for her," said Lulu sadly.

The Pony Pals were still making hats when Eve came back to the kitchen. She held out a rolled up piece of paper tied with red ribbon. "It's your present," she said.

Pam smiled at Eve as she accepted the gift. Eve smiled back, but her eyes were red. Pam could tell she'd been crying.

"Thank you, Eve," said Anna.

"We'll wait until the party to open it," added Lulu.

"I want you to open it now," said Eve.

"Shouldn't we wait until the party?" asked Pam. "When you open your present."

Eve shook her head no.

Pam and Anna exchanged a glance. They were both worried about Eve.

"Okay," Pam told Eve. "We'll open it."

Pam untied the ribbon, unrolled the paper and spread it out in the middle of the table. The Pony Pals looked at it together.

It was a letter. Tears sprang to Pam's eyes as she read it.

Dear Pony Pals,

I have a present for you.
It is Lucky. I can't take
care of him. You will love
him and train him. He'll
play with your ponies.
Please let Lucky be a
pony pal.
Your friend,
    Eve.

69

Pam looked around at Lulu and Anna. They were shocked by Eve's gift, too. They needed three ideas. And fast.

"Don't you like your present?" asked Eve. Her voice was choked with tears. "It's Lucky. He's the present."

"But Lucky is your pony, Eve," said Anna. "You love him so much."

"I can't train him by myself," said Eve. "So my mom and dad won't let me keep him."

"I know," admitted Pam.

Anna and Lulu nodded that they knew, too.

"He's happy here," continued Eve. "And you can train him."

"I have an idea," said Pam. "Maybe you could

board him here with the ponies and horses in our barns. We'd train him for free. Your parents would only have to pay for boarding."

"When he's trained you can take him back," said Lulu.

"You mean he'd still be my pony?" asked Eve.

"He'd be *only* your pony. We'd just be his teachers," said Pam.

"And you could come and visit whenever you wanted," said Lulu. "Wiggins isn't so far from Edison. You could help train Lucky."

"And go for trail rides with us," added Anna. "On Daisy."

"You're a good rider," Pam told her. "And when Lucky grows up and is all trained, he can go home with you."

Eve's sad expression was slowly turning into a happier one. Anna put a red party hat on Eve's head.

"You'd be a Junior Pony Pal," said Lulu. "Like Mimi and Rosalie."

Eve grinned at the Pony Pals. "Thank you," she said.

"It's a perfect solution," said Lulu.

It's perfect, thought Pam, if my mother agrees and the Greeleys will let Lucky board here. Those were two big *ifs*.

Party Time

"I'm going to find my mother," Pam told Eve, Lulu and Anna. "And tell her our idea about Lucky."

"We'll stay here and finish making hats for the party," said Lulu.

"And decorate the cake," added Eve. "That's the yummy job."

Pam hoped her mother would let Lucky stay. I'll promise to take care of him, thought Pam as she ran into the barn.

Mrs. Crandal was in the tack room cleaning a bridle. She listened carefully to the Pony Pal plan for Lucky and Eve. She agreed that it was a good idea.

"Do you think Eve's mom and dad will say it's okay?" asked Pam.

"I don't know," answered Mrs. Crandal. "I hope so. For Eve's sake."

When Pam came back to the kitchen, Eve and the twins were busy decorating the cake with pink and silver sprinkles.

Pam motioned Lulu and Anna to the other side of the kitchen. She told them that her mother said Lucky could be a boarder. "Now we have to convince Eve's parents that it's a good idea," she said.

"How?" asked Lulu.

"Let's show them how much fun Eve has here," suggested Anna.

"The party is perfect for that," said Lulu.

"She should ride Daisy when they're here," added Pam. "That will show them how good she is with ponies."

"We should show them that Lucky is making progress, too," said Anna.

"They'll see him with Lightning," said Pam. "And we'll explain how he's being trained."

"Let's bring Eve to the barn and start grooming the ponies for the party," suggested Lulu.

The four girls ran to the barn. Eve took Pam's hand. "I'm going to come here *every* week," she said happily.

If your parents agree to our plan, thought Pam.

An hour later the four ponies were groomed. Lightning and Lucky were in the small paddock. Snow White and Acorn were in the big paddock. The Pony Pals, Eve and the Crandal twins waited near the paddock for Mimi and Rosalie.

Lulu pointed across the big field. "Here they come," she announced. "They're coming on Pony Pal Trail."

Mrs. Bell and Rosalie led Tongo. Mimi sat proudly in the saddle.

"Tongo's so cute!" exclaimed Jill. "Come on, Eve."

Eve and the twins ran ahead. The Pony Pals followed.

"Happy birthday to Lucky," shouted Mimi.

Pam introduced Eve to Mimi, Rosalie, Mrs. Bell and Tongo.

Rosalie held out a bunch of carrots with a big, yellow ribbon tied around the green ends. "I have a present for your pony," she told Eve.

"Thanks," said Eve. "He'll love them."

Eve took the carrots from Rosalie. At that instant, Tongo stretched his neck and bit off a carrot.

They all laughed.

"Tongo wants treats all the time," said Mimi.

"So does Lucky," said Eve.

"Here's another present for him," said Mimi. "It's for you and Lucky. I made it."

Mimi handed Eve a big envelope.

Eve opened the envelope and pulled out a hand-made prize ribbon with a big #1 on it.

"Lucky is Number One today because it's his birthday," said Mimi. "He's the birthday boy all day long."

"Thank you," said Eve. "It's his first ribbon."

"That's a terrific present," Lulu told Mimi. She turned to Rosalie. "So are the carrots."

The party moved over to the paddock. Lucky cantered up to the fence to meet Tongo. The two ponies sniffed one another over the fence. Lucky perked up his ears.

"He loves other ponies," said Eve.

Pam looked at her watch. Mr. and Mrs. Greeley would be there any minute. "Time to open our present, Eve," said Pam.

Lulu handed Eve a gift-wrapped box. Anna had drawn running ponies all over the wrapping. "The paper's so pretty," said Eve. "I'm going to keep it."

"Open it," said Jack. "I want to see."

Eve carefully unwrapped the box, opened it and looked inside.

"Gloves!" she exclaimed. "Riding gloves. They're so great."

Eve put the gloves on. They fitted her perfectly. "I love them," she said.

Pam noticed the Greeleys pulling into the driveway.

Lulu saw them, too. "Eve, let's go and get Daisy ready for riding," she suggested. "I'll help you saddle her up."

"Can I ride, too?" asked Rosalie.

"You can ride Acorn," said Anna. "But you have to help Lulu saddle him up."

"I will," exclaimed Rosalie. "I love to do that."

"Anna and I will go and meet your parents," said Pam. She exchanged a glance with Anna. It was their job to tell Eve's parents their plan.

Lulu, Eve and the party guests went to get Daisy and Acorn. Pam and Anna ran across the yard to meet the Greeleys.

First, Pam told Eve's parents about Lucky's training. Then Anna told them that Lightning was teaching Lucky, too.

"Can Eve train Lucky by herself now?" asked Mrs. Greeley.

"No," answered Pam truthfully. "But we have an idea."

Pam told Eve's parents that the Pony Pals would take care of Lucky, but that Eve should come once a week to help.

Mr. and Mrs. Greeley turned to one another.

"It will mean that one of us has to drive over here every weekend," Mrs. Greeley said.

"We could do our weekly shopping at the

Wiggins Green Market," said Mr. Greeley. "It's one of the best in the area."

"And have lunch at that great diner," suggested Mrs. Greeley.

"Or go for a hike," added Mr. Greeley. "That would be a nice way to spend a weekend afternoon."

"Where is Eve?" asked Mrs. Greeley.

Anna told them that Eve was riding Daisy. "Let's go and see her ride," suggested Pam.

Pam and Anna walked with Eve's parents to the riding ring. Lulu and Mrs. Crandal were in the center of the ring. Eve and Rosalie were cantering their ponies. Mrs. Bell, Mimi and Tongo watched. When Eve saw her mother and father she halted the pony and walked her over to them.

"This is Daisy," Eve told her parents. "I can ride her any time. I'm a Junior Pony Pal."

"Pam and Anna have asked us already if Lucky can board here," said Mrs. Greeley.

"Can he?" begged Eve. "And I can come and take care of him sometimes. I can be a Pony Pal. A *Junior* Pony Pal."

"Just like me and Mimi," said Rosalie.

"Yes," said her mother. "You can."

"I can! I can!" shouted Eve. "Thank you! Thank you!"

Lucky ran up to the paddock fence and nickered as if to say, "What's all the excitement?" Lightning followed him.

Anna started singing happy birthday to Lucky. Everyone joined in.

When the song was over, Pam went up to Lightning and scratched her forehead. "Good work, Lightning," she said. "You found Lucky for us after the accident. And you're helping to train him."

Pam kissed her pony's cheek. "I love you," she whispered.

Dear Pony Pal:

There are now Pony Pals all over the United States, Australia, New Zealand, Canada, Germany and Norway.

When I first started writing the Pony Pals I thought there would only be six books. Now there are twenty-six books. I am surprised that I have so many stories to tell about Pam, Anna, Lulu and their ponies. They are like real people, who keep having adventures that I want to write down for them.

When I am not writing Pony Pal or CHEER USA books, I like to swim, hike, draw and paint. I also like to visit horse farms and talk to people who love and ride ponies and horses. I don't ride anymore and have never owned my own pony or horse. But my husband and I have two young cats, Lucca and Todi. They are brothers and get along great with our old dog, Willie.

It's wonderful to know that so many Pony Pals from different parts of the world enjoy the adventures of Pam, Anna, Lulu, Lightning, Acorn and Snow White. I think about you when I am writing. A special thankyou to those who have written me letters and sent drawings and photos. I love your drawings of ponies and keep your photos on the wall near my computer. They inspire me to write more Pony Pal stories.

Remember, you don't need a pony to be a Pony Pal.

Happy Reading,

Jeanne Betancourt